GRAFFIX

First paperback edition 1997
Reprinted 1997, 1998, 1999

First published 1997 in hardback by
A & C Black (Publishers) Ltd
35 Bedford Row, London WC1R 4JH

Text copyright © 1997 Anthony Masters
Illustrations copyright © 1997 Gary Rees
Cover illustration © 1998 Peter Dennis

The right of Anthony Masters to be identified as author
of this work has been asserted by him in accordance
with the Copyrights, Designs and Patents Act 1988.

ISBN 0-7136-4711-6

A CIP catalogue for this book is available from
the British Library.

Printed in Great Britain by William Clowes Ltd,
Beccles, Suffolk.

Biker

Anthony Masters

Illustrated by Gary Rees

A & C Black · London

The author is grateful to the Strudwick Family and Guy Farbrother for their expert advice about moto-cross.

Chapter One

Terry was high up on the wall that ran round the school playground, balancing on one leg while the rest of the kids yelled and clapped.

Go for it, Tel.

But as he climbed down, triumphant, Mr Benson, the Head Teacher, came out of his office and walked slowly towards him. The crowd scattered.

Terry knew he was going to be in big trouble. The school wall had chunks of glass along the top and no one was allowed to climb it.

As Terry walked home, Mr Benson's letter felt as if it was red hot and burning a huge hole in his pocket. Terry knew that he couldn't have picked a worse moment to get into trouble. He'd been hoping to persuade his dad to come and watch him in his next bike race, but now he was sure that he wouldn't come.

Why had he been so stupid? Dad was going to be furious.

Terry was right. As soon as his dad read Mr Benson's letter, he lost his temper.

What on earth's the matter with you? Your brother Jon never got into trouble like this.

I'm fed up with it. All you *do* is make a fool of yourself.

Terry remained silent. He knew that whatever he said, it would only make things worse.

When his dad had finished, he went upstairs, feeling sorry for himself. Being the youngest wasn't easy, particularly when he got into so many scrapes, but in his heart of hearts Terry also knew that he showed off for a reason. He wanted people to notice him because his dad never seemed to. He only noticed Jon.

11

Chapter Two

The spray rose high in the air as Terry's bike roared through the water and then up the muddy hillside track which got steeper all the time.

He could hardly see through his goggles, but he knew he wasn't going to come off at the corner. Terry was too confident for that.

He might not be much good at lessons or games, but moto-cross was his sport and he was going to win the Harker Cup.

He was up on top of the hill now, ahead of the others, his bike rearing and snorting like a horse. He gazed down at the final run.

The jump came up at him fast, and Terry revved his bike as much as he could. He pulled back hard, dragging on the handlebars and keeping the front wheel off the ground.

Then he made a fatal mistake. Thinking he'd got
the race sewn up, he allowed himself to relax
a little. He looked up at the crowd ahead,
and for a split second he thought he saw
his dad and felt a rush of happiness.
But when he looked more closely he
realised it wasn't his dad after all, just
someone who looked like him.

He tried to regain his balance
but it was too late. His wheel
dropped, and as the bike
flipped over Terry was
thrown to the ground.

Mum took Terry's mud-spattered helmet and handed him a drink.

Bad luck. Are you OK?

Terry was too busy checking his bike for damage to reply.

Just then, Steve and his mates strolled up. Steve had always been jealous of Terry. He was sixteen, and he hated being beaten by a twelve-year-old kid who only had a fourth-hand bike. Steve's mates gazed at Terry with jubilant grins.

Bent your fuel tank, haven't you?

Pity about that brake cable.

There's nothing that can't be fixed.

Come on, Terry, we've got to get going.

Steve and his mates slouched away into the crowd,
but not before Terry heard Ronnie say,

As they drove home, Terry wished once again that he hadn't been caught showing off at school. Then his dad might really have been watching him instead of standing shouting on the touchline at Jon's stupid rugby match. Terry thought about the Harker Cup. He <u>had</u> to win his section in that.

But that wasn't good enough for Terry.

Sometimes he really hated Jon, and he was sure now he was his father's favourite.

Chapter Three

A week later, Terry waited on the start line for
the practice run, with half a dozen other
riders, all revving their engines.
Each of them knew that whoever came out
of the first corner ahead had a good
chance of winning the race.
It was all a question of courage.

With a roar they were off down the hill, the mud flying, the bend coming up fast. Terry gunned his bike's engine, standing up to soften the bumps. Willing himself on, he inched slightly ahead. Then they were into the corner, trying to balance, jockeying for position, the bikes so close they were almost touching.

Terry was pressurising the boy alongside him. At the moment they were neck and neck. Someone had to give way and he was sure that it wasn't going to be him. He hung on until the boy lost his nerve and came off the accelerator. Then Terry was past him.

The rest of the course was easy. Terry was up front all the way and soared over the last jump, his bike like some incredible flying machine.

Steve and his mates were on the fringe of the crowd and Terry could see them skulking away, not wanting to share in his success. Steve hadn't even bothered to practise. Was that because he was frightened of being shown up again?

23

At supper, Terry asked his dad about the race.

I'll come to the Harker. But I'll have to go on to Jon's match.

Kill two birds with one stone?

He does his best. It's a long way between Tigley and Burton.

Mum frowned at Terry but he took no notice.

You can watch Jon playing any time, Dad. This is my big one. The Harker Cup. You've got to see the whole race.

I'll come.

'I was asking Dad,' said Terry. He knew he was hurting Sue but he was anxious to put his father on the spot.

Jon found his brother's resentment difficult to handle.
Jon was good-looking - tall and thin with blond
hair. He was good at sport, a hard worker
and an excellent all-rounder. Terry was
short and stocky. He often wanted
to be like his older brother,
but he would never
admit it.

I don't mind
if you go and
watch Terry.

'Thanks for the favour,'
muttered Terry, not
wanting to be
patronised.

I'll try and see part
of it. I can't do much more
without actually splitting
myself in half, can I?

Grinning wickedly, Terry picked up a baked bean and flicked it at Jon. The bean hit him on the tip of his nose, leaving a red smear. Jon stood up, fists clenched.

I'll get you.

But Terry was already running upstairs.

He slammed the door and lay on his bed, burying his head in the pillow. Dad would never come to the meeting now. Why had he blown it again? It was almost as if he <u>wanted</u> Dad to dislike him.

A few minutes later there was a knock on Terry's bedroom door.

Go away, Sue.

It's not Sue. It's Dad. Can I come in?

Mr Trent knew how Terry felt about Jon and he wanted to try and reassure him. He also had the feeling that his youngest son was determined to test him out, see how far he would let him go.

Nervously, Mr Trent tried to talk to Terry. 'Look. Jon's <u>not</u> my favourite. It's just that you're not making it easy for yourself or me. You keep winding Jon up and upsetting your sister and getting into trouble at school. You've got to snap out of it, Terry. Then we can make a fresh start.'

Terry wasn't prepared to be the villain of the family. He turned on his side so that his dad wouldn't see the tears in his eyes.

It's not fair. Leave me alone. Just leave me alone.

Chapter Four

At last the day of the race for the Harker Cup came
and Terry was very nervous. Dad had arrived and
seemed to be staying and Terry was desperate to win.
The marshals were already in place and the riders
were revving up.

'Take short cuts through the wood, Dad.
Then you can see how I'm doing,'
Terry suggested, as he gave his
bike a final check.

'I'll have to be pretty nippy to do that,' replied Mr
Trent, but he was grinning. Terry still hoped he'd
stay for the whole race. Surely he would.

When Steve had gone, Mr Trent snapped,

I don't think much of him.

He's all right really, Dad. He's just a bit of a big mouth.

Mr Trent turned and muttered something to his wife. Terry strained his ears, and despite the revving of the bikes caught the words, 'mixing with the wrong crowd'.

Terry jostled for position at the first corner, drawing ahead, the sweat running down his face. The bike roared over the bumpy track, skidding in the mud as he stood up on the foot rest.

Then, to his horror, Terry saw Steve coming up on the inside. He's going to take me, he thought. Sure enough, Steve drew ahead. He was grinning.

Terry gunned the accelerator up the hill and then began to weave down the woodland track. He knew where he had to ease off the throttle as he tried to out-wit the other riders. He had to close the gap between himself and Steve.

'Mixing with the wrong crowd' - his father's words echoed in his mind, and they made him even more determined to win.

As he went for the downhill descent and the final corner, Terry concentrated hard. He had to overtake Steve. He had to overtake him now. He was squeezing the throttle so tightly that his hand was rigid. He was determined to make Steve lose his nerve as they both skidded round the corner.

Suddenly Terry squeezed past him with a wild cry of triumph. Mud and water shot up all around him as he roared over the last jump, flying high in the air. Then he bumped to the ground and stood up in his saddle as he crossed the finish line.

He had won. The Harker Cup was his. Everyone was clapping and cheering, Mum yelling louder than the rest. But where was his father? He couldn't see him anywhere.

Well done, Terry.

'Where's Dad? He didn't see me win,' Terry muttered, all his triumph fading away.

'You've got to learn to share with Jon, Terry,' his mother replied. 'It's only fair. You're making it impossible for Dad. He doesn't want to upset you.'

He was about to reply when Steve appeared. 'Well done, Tel.' He was smiling with everything but his eyes. 'You took me. Proud of your little boy are you, Mrs T?'

Of course. What happened to you then, Steven?

Switched off, didn't I?

He walked hurriedly away.

Terry put his hands in his pockets and slouched away to the snack bar. A few minutes later he arrived back, munching a hot-dog. He looked round for his bike but he couldn't see it anywhere. He stared around in amazement.

41

Terry began to panic, and when his mother returned, picking her way slowly through the mud, he ran to meet her.

MY BIKE'S GONE.

'It must be around here somewhere,' she snapped, feeling tired and wanting to go home.

Terry's voice shook. 'Someone's nicked it.'

43

Lee said one was stolen last week and it was found burnt out on a rubbish dump.

There were tears in Terry's eyes. He had spent months saving up for the bike and it was more than just a possession. His bike had made him a winner.

'It wasn't found burnt out. I've heard that rumour before,' said the policeman. 'It's still missing. Some of these bikes are worth quite a bit. Once they're stolen they can be taken to another county and sold.'

Terry shrugged her off and ran back towards the track. The bike had to be there somewhere. However sorry Mum was, she couldn't afford to buy him another bike. Neither could Dad.

Steve was sitting by the track with Ronnie and Scott.

What you looking for, Tel?

My bike. You seen it?

No way. You didn't go off and leave it, did you?

Only for a minute.

Terry felt very stupid.

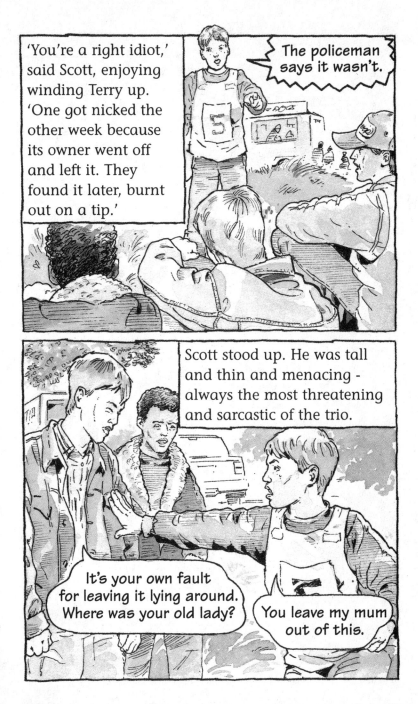

'You're a right idiot,' said Scott, enjoying winding Terry up. 'One got nicked the other week because its owner went off and left it. They found it later, burnt out on a tip.'

The policeman says it wasn't.

Scott stood up. He was tall and thin and menacing - always the most threatening and sarcastic of the trio.

It's your own fault for leaving it lying around. Where was your old lady?

You leave my mum out of this.

Then an idea flashed across Terry's mind. Suppose <u>they'd</u> taken his bike out of spite, because he'd beaten Steve.

Let's have a look in your van.

Derek Reid took it home. We're going to a rave tonight in Ronnie's car.

Terry didn't care how big Steve was. He'd *kill* him if he'd taken his bike.

In a sudden rage, he swung his helmet at Scott. The heavy surface made contact with Scott's knuckles and he howled in pain while the others looked on laughing.

Scott grabbed the helmet and hit him hard round the side of the neck. Terry fought back, kicking and punching until Scott thumped him hard in the stomach. He went down on the ground, winded and gasping.

'What's happened?' she cried, horrified to find Terry gasping for air.

That lot nicked my bike.

Did they say so?

No, but I know they did. It's in Scott's van and his mate's driven it away.

The policeman pushed his way through the rapidly growing crowd.

Now what's going on?

Terry began to explain.

Chapter Five

Even Jon was sympathetic when Terry arrived home.
Mr Trent took charge of the situation immediately.

I'll ring the police right away and get this sorted out.

Pleased that his father was being such a support, Terry felt much better. Maybe the police <u>would</u> find his bike in the back of Scott's van after all.

But an hour later the police phoned and told Terry's dad that they had checked the van but found it empty.

They must have sold it.

The police have done what they can. Those boys may be troublemakers, but that doesn't mean they stole your bike.

'I know they did,' muttered Terry. 'Steve wanted to get at me.'

That doesn't mean he stole your bike. I have to say I think it was careless to leave it lying around. I know you were excited about winning, but –

You didn't even know I'd won!

Terry was standing up and shouting, all his bitterness spilling out. 'You didn't care.'

He went out and slammed the door.

55

Terry lay on his bed feeling lonely and miserable. His bike had gone for good and he wouldn't be able to ride for the rest of the season - if at all. It had taken him over a year to save up. What was he going to do?

He lay there waiting, but Dad didn't come.
The next day was Sunday and Terry stayed in bed.
At ten o'clock there was a knock at the door.

I'm taking Jon and Sue down to the pool. They'd like you to come and so would I.

He was trying very hard to be friendly.

All right. But I'm <u>not</u> swimming, and I'm not going without breakfast.

'It's all ready for you,' snapped his father, turning to go downstairs. 'But we can't wait all day.'

Terry was silent in the car, determined not to speak to anyone.

If your bike doesn't turn up, I'll help you with the money. I'm going to go strawberry picking this summer and –

You won't have any spare money. You'll need all you can get for college.

Moments later, out of the corner of his eye, Terry saw Steve on his road bike. He was trying to pass the car whilst giving him a rude sign at the same time.

Mr Trent had seen him now and his grip on the steering wheel tightened.

Isn't that the boy at the track? The idiot's trying to overtake us on a bend. Your friend, isn't he?

He's not my friend.

Steve gunned his bike past the car, a triumphant smile on his face. But his smile didn't last long. A truck came round the corner at speed and Steve skidded towards them, his lips parted in terror.

Horrified, Terry watched his dad swerve, wrestling with the wheel as a telephone box reared up in front of them.

KRUMP

Amidst the sound of crunching metal and a shower of shattering glass, the car came to a grinding halt.

Are you OK?

There was a long silence, broken by Steve tapping on the side window. Terry tugged open the back door and clambered out on to the pavement. Jon and Sue were still inside, looking shocked, but uninjured.

Then Terry noticed the blood streaming down his father's forehead.

'Quick,' he shouted at Steve. 'Help me get the door open.' 'Dad's injured.'

The boys tugged at the door as a crowd began to gather.

Look what you've done to my dad.

'You carved us up, Steve,' accused Terry. His father looked terribly still.

It was an accident. It'll be all right, you'll see.

No, it won't be all right. And it was your fault.

He pushed Steve aside.

To his great relief, his father stirred and opened his eyes, but the blood was still pouring down his face.

The truck driver ran across the road to them, clutching a mobile phone.

Terry forced himself not to panic, but he knew he had to stop the blood fast. Taking off his tee shirt, he ripped it into two pieces and rolled one into a pad, applying it firmly to his father's head.

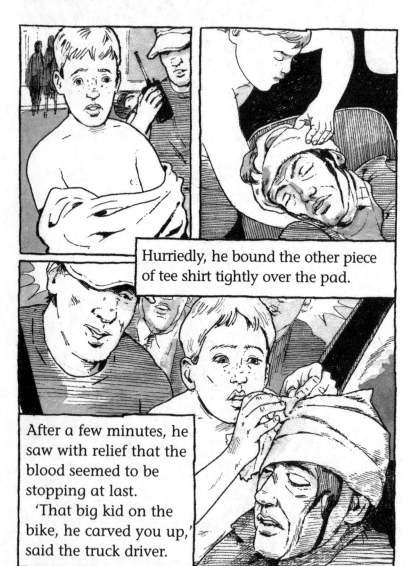

Hurriedly, he bound the other piece of tee shirt tightly over the pad.

After a few minutes, he saw with relief that the blood seemed to be stopping at last.

'That big kid on the bike, he carved you up,' said the truck driver.

69

The journey to the hospital was tense. Sue and Jon were still in shock, while Terry stared fearfully down at his father. Had he got his first aid right? Was Dad going to recover?

After a routine check-up, Terry, Jon and Sue were sent home, but Mr Trent was kept in overnight. The gash in his head needed stitches and the doctor wanted to keep an eye on him.

The police had taken statements, but Terry knew his dad wasn't going to make things worse for Steve than they already were. He had heard him telling the police that Steve had taken 'a bit of a risk'. It was a generous statement, thought Terry.
Too generous.

Before he left for home, Terry went up to the ward to find his dad. He was sitting up in bed, reading a newspaper. He had a bandage round his head and was still looking pale and shaken.

'Where did you learn the first aid?' Dad asked at once. 'At the moto-cross?'

Terry nodded.

They grinned shyly at each other. There was a lot of ground to make up, but for the first time in ages Terry knew that his father loved him.

Chapter Six

Terry, Jon and Sue were given the next day off school in which to recover from the shock of the crash. Halfway through the morning, while his mother had gone to bring his dad home, Terry received a telephone call.

Dad came down the path just as Terry was setting out for the station. He looked much better.

I've just had a call, but I don't know who made it. They said my bike's down at the station. I'm going to get it.

Was it Steve?

I don't think so.

Hang on. I'll come with you.

You need a rest.

Rest? Who wants a rest? This is important.

He put his arm round Terry's shoulders and they set off together to collect the bike.

When they arrived at the station, Terry saw his bike leaning up against the wall, covered in mud but otherwise completely unharmed.

His father went round to the booking office to identify Terry's bike. He also explained about the telephone call at the same time.

That's weird. Why didn't they just chuck it away somewhere?

'They must have known you,' replied Dad slowly. 'Maybe they thought it was more valuable than it was. And by the way - neither of their descriptions fits Steve.'

Why should they ring me then?

'Could be they felt sorry for you,' said Dad. 'Could be they even had a change of heart. People aren't <u>all</u> out to get you, you know.'

I used to think they were.

Chapter Seven

Terry revved his bike, opened the throttle and roared down the valley, the mud splattering about him and the wind like music in his ears. All the winners of the Harker Cup did a lap of honour and now it was his turn. Although he had no competition, Terry was determined to put everything he could into it.

He pulled back on his handlebars and his front wheel left the ground, taking the jump and soaring right up into the air. Then he was down again with a thump, keeping his balance and zooming towards the flag. His dad stood there, clapping proudly, and Terry had never felt so happy.

But as he skidded to a halt, a great shower of muddy water swept over his father who had been standing too close to the track.

Sorry.

It's all right. What's a little mud between friends?